This Walker book belongs to:

....

....

....

For Josie

First published 1993 by Walker Books Ltd
87 Vauxhall Walk, London SE11 5HJ

This edition published 2013

2 4 6 8 10 9 7 5 3 1

© 1993 Lucy Cousins

Lucy Cousins Font © 2013

The right of Lucy Cousins to be identified as author/illustrator of this work
has been asserted by her in accordance with the Copyright, Designs and Patents Act 1988

This book has been typeset in Palatino with Tiepolo punctuation

Printed in China

British Library Cataloguing in Publication Data:
a catalogue record for this book is available from the British Library

ISBN 978-1-4063-4500-1

www.walker.co.uk

Noah's Ark

Retold and illustrated by

Lucy Cousins

WALKER BOOKS
AND SUBSIDIARIES
LONDON · BOSTON · SYDNEY · AUCKLAND

A long time ago there lived
a man called Noah.
Noah was a good man,
who trusted in God.

There were also many wicked people in the world. God wanted to punish the wicked people, so he said to Noah ...

"I shall make

and wash all

Build an

and all

a flood of Water
the Wicked people away.
ark for your family
the animals."

Noah worked

for years

and years

and years ...

to build the ark.

At last the ark was finished.

Noah and his family
gathered lots of food.

Then the animals came,
two by two ...

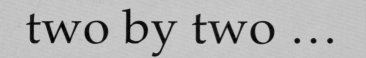

two by two ...

into the ark.

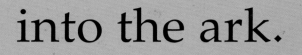

When the ark was full
Noah felt a drop of rain.

It rained

and rained

and rained.

It rained ...

for forty days and forty nights.

The world was covered
with water.

At last the rain stopped
and the sun came out.
Noah sent a dove to
find dry land.

The dove came back with
a leafy twig.
"Hurrah!" shouted Noah.
"The flood has ended."

But many more days passed before the ark came to rest on dry land.

Then Noah and all
the animals came
safely out of
the ark ...

and life began again on the earth.

Lucy Cousins

is the multi-award-winning creator of much-loved character Maisy.
She has written and illustrated over 100 books and has sold
over 25 million copies worldwide.

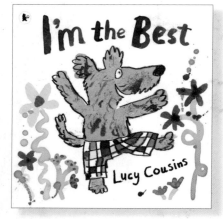

978-1-4063-2872-1

978-1-4063-4392-2

978-1-4063-3838-6

978-1-4063-2965-0

978-1-4063-3579-8

978-1-4063-4501-8

978-1-4063-4510-0

Available from all good booksellers

www.walker.co.uk